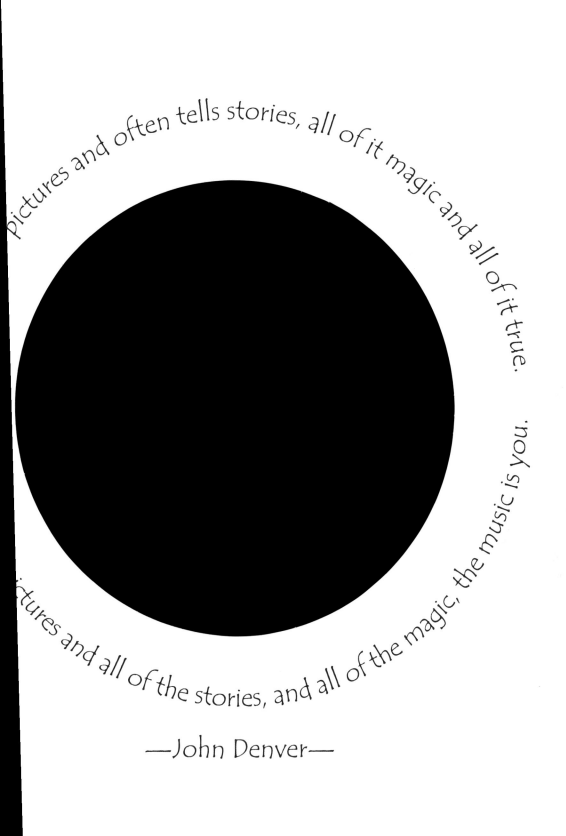

pictures and often tells stories, all of it magic and all of it true.

...tures and all of the stories, and all of the magic, the music is you.

...ictures and all of the stories, and all of the magic, the music is you.

—John Denver—

For Keira, Love, NeeNee

Many thanks to children's literary agent Sandy Ferguson Fuller of Alp Arts Company, who, while John Denver was alive, conceiv
John's spirit to children through picture books, and after his passing pursued it to fruition; also to Hal Thau, John's long-time friend
Jim Bell of Bell Licensing; and Michael Connelly and Keith Hauprich of Cherry Lane Music Publishing Compa

A Sharing Nature With Children Book

DAWN PUBLICATIONS
12402 Bitney Springs Road
Nevada City, California 95959
www.dawnpub.com

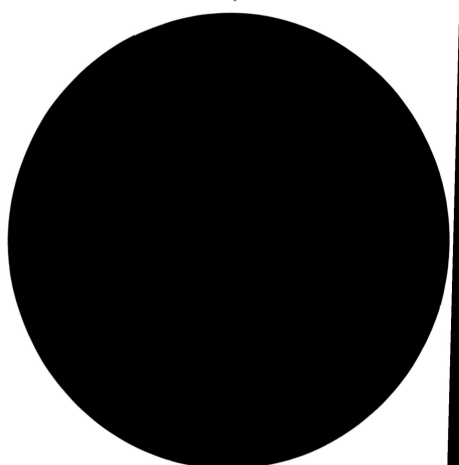

Library of Congress Cataloging-in-Publicati
Denver, John.
 John Denver's For baby (for Bobbie) / ada
Mason. -- 1st ed.
   p. cm. -- (John Denver & kids series)
 "A sharing nature with children book."
 Summary: A picture book adaptation of Jc
as a love song and has also been interpreted
love for a child. Includes facts about Denve
       ISBN 978-1-58469-120-4 (hardback)
     1. Children's songs--United States--Te
        Songs.] I. Mason, Janeen I., ill. II
                                     Bobbi
                           PZ8.3.D436
                            782.42--
                              [E]

Design and computer production by Patty Arnold, *Menagerie Design and Publishing*
First Edition
10 9 8 7 6 5 4 3 2 1
Printed in China

John Denver's

For Baby
(For Bobbie)

Adapted and illustrated by Janeen Mason

DAWN PUBLICATIONS

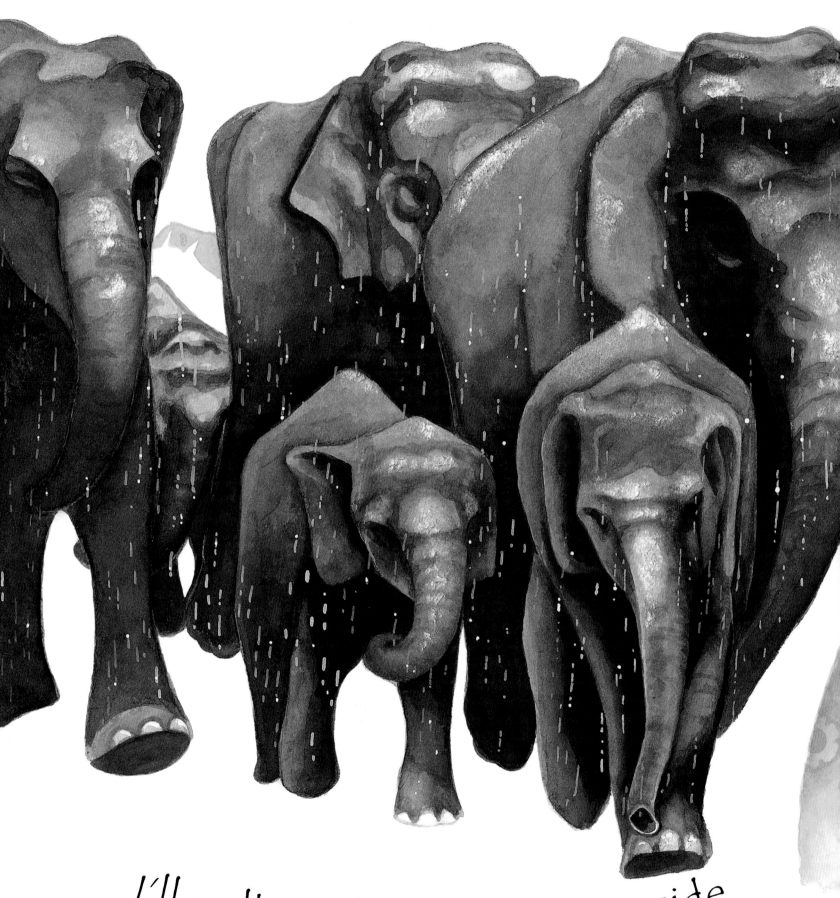

I'll walk in the rain by your side,

I'll cling to the warmth of your hand.

I'll love you more than anybody can.

And the wind will whisper your name to me,

Little birds will sing along in time.

Leaves will bow down
when you walk by,

And morning bells will chime.

I'll be there when you're feelin' down,
To kiss away the fears if you cry.

A reflection of the love in your eyes.

And I'll sing you the songs of the rainbow,
A whisper of the joy that is mine.

And leaves will
bow down
when you walk by,

And morning bells will chime.

I'll walk in the rain by your side,

I'll do anything to help you understand,
I'll love you more than anybody can.

And the wind will whisper your name to me,
Little birds will sing along in time,

Leaves will bow down when you walk by,
And morning bells will chime.

About the Animals and Where They Live

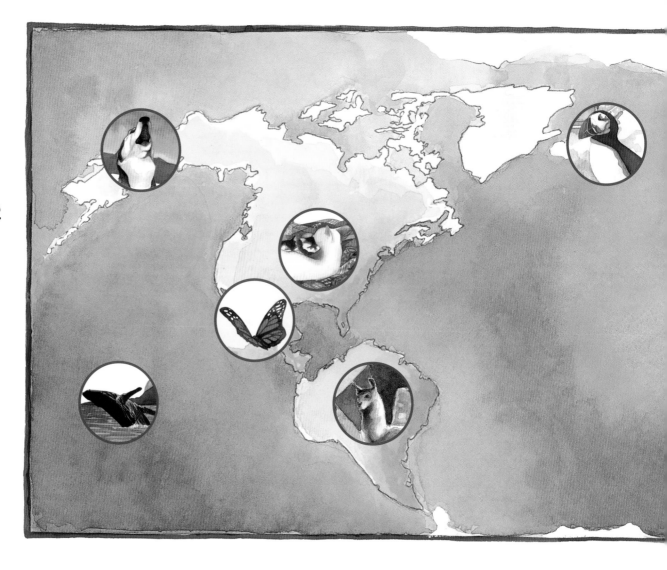

In **SRI LANKA**, if an *elephant* calf loses its mother it can live at the Pinnawela Elephant Orphanage, where elephants play in the river every day. An elephant baby weighs about 300 pounds and stands 3 feet tall when it's born, but when grown can weigh 10,000 pounds and stand 10 feet tall.

The *kangaroo* is native to **AUSTRALIA**, and it can move very fast by hopping on two powerful legs. A baby is called a "joey," and when born is only as big as a jelly bean. For the first ten months, joeys stay safe, warm, and fed in the mother's pouch. A fully grown kangaroo stands 6 feet tall and weighs about 200 pounds.

In **ICELAND** when a baby *puffin* is big enough to leave its cliff-side nest forever, it waits until after dark to try to fly to the nearby ocean. But some get confused and head toward the lights of a town instead. Schools close during this time of year so children can stay up late to rescue the wayward "pufflings" and release them at sunrise into the sea.

In **ENGLAND**, injured *hedgehogs* go to the world's busiest wildlife hospital, a place called Tiggywinkles after the famous character from Beatrix Potter's books. Over 10,000 animals are treated there for free every year.

All over **AMERICA**, The Humane Society keeps *cats* and *kittens*, as well as puppies and dogs, warm, clean and fed until they can be adopted by a "forever family." Humane societies teach children and adults the importance of respect, compassion, and responsibility in the treatment of animals and their habitats.

In the summer, *humpback whales* live in cold polar waters where they eat lots of krill and small fish, and build up layers of fat. In the winter, they head for warmer places like the ocean around **HAWAII**, where the mothers give birth. A newborn calf can be 20 feet long and weigh 4,000 pounds. The babies drink lots of mother's milk—but they are the only ones eating! Adults fast all winter long, living off their fat.

Siberian huskies have two coats of fur. The inner coat is short and soft while the outer coat is longer and more stiff. The layers insulate them when the temperature in the **ARTIC** drops to as low as –76 degrees F.

In the fall, *monarch butterflies* migrate from eastern and central U.S. to **MEXICO** where they "overwinter," blanketing trees—the same trees, every year—by the millions. When the weather warms they migrate north again. But monarchs born in the summer live only 2 to 3 weeks. Those that migrate the following winter may well be five generations removed from those that migrated the previous winter. How they learn the route is a mystery.

Baby *baboons* in **EAST AFRICA** hang onto their mother's belly for the first month, cling to her back for the next few months, and when they're four to six months old they sit up as they ride. Baboons can live through drought by licking the dew from their fur in the mornings.

Giant panda bears live in the remote mountains of central **CHINA**. The only thing they eat is bamboo, which is not very nourishing, so they have to eat a lot of it—about 28 pounds a day! Babies are hairless, blind and tiny when born—only 3 to 4 ounces—but will grow to over 200 pounds.

Surefooted *llamas* are domesticated animals native to the Andes Mountains of **PERU**. Their wool is woven into colorful, warm blankets. They also carry food and supplies up the rugged paths high into the mountains. A baby llama, called a "cria," weighs 25 pounds at birth. A fully grown llama is about 6 feet tall and 325 pounds.

Orangutans are great apes that live in the rainforest canopy of **BORNEO** and **SUMATRA**. They are known for being very intelligent. At night they make nests high above ground which they cover with an umbrella of leaves to keep them dry. Their strong arms reach seven feet, which allows them to travel great distances by swinging arm over arm through the trees.

For Baby (For Bobbie)

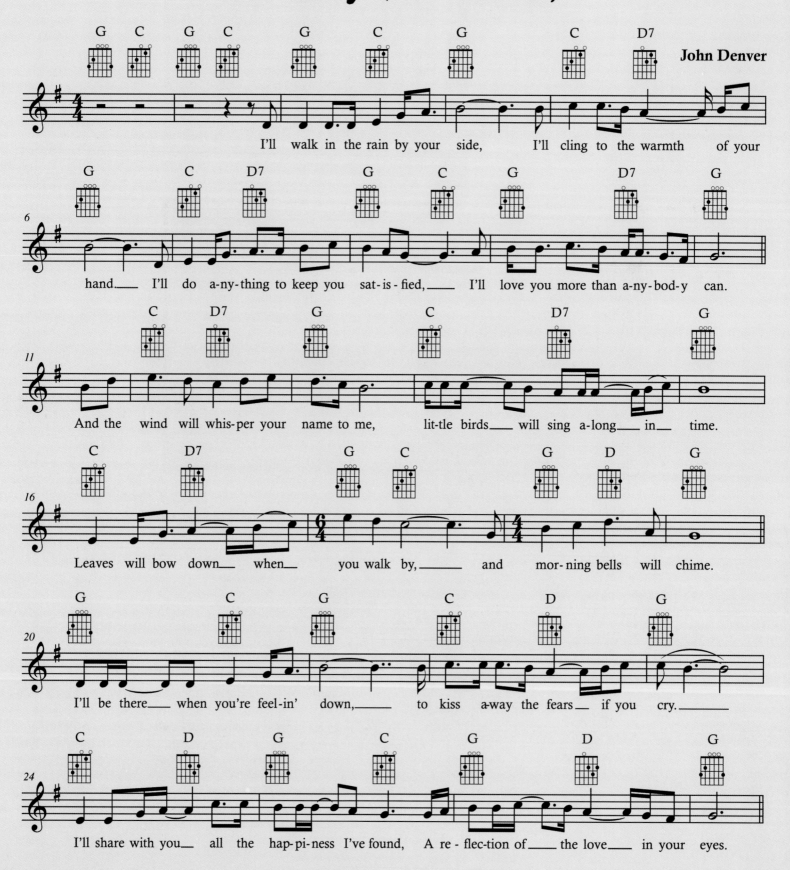

John Denver

This is one of the first songs that John Denver ever wrote, and the first of his songs that he recorded. The song is simultaneously a love song in the romantic sense, and a love song to a child. As John explains:

It was written for a girl named Bobbie, who I had fallen in love with once upon a time, when I was first starting out in the world and trying to do something with my music. . . . Mary Travers (of Peter, Paul & Mary) heard it differently, and sang it as a love song for her daughter. It's great that a song can be appreciated on different levels like that. So, it's 'For Bobbie'—a love song between a man and a woman (not quite yet a man and a woman), and 'For Baby'—a love song from a woman to a newborn child. How wonderful.

John's grandmother gave him his first guitar at the age of seven, and another at the age of twelve. He loved to sing and play, and by the 1970s John Denver was one of America's most

John Denver's adopted son Zak gets a ride.

popular musicians. Several of his songs reached #1 on the charts. Over 32 million John Denver albums have sold in the United States alone, making him one of the top selling vocal artists of all time. Yet John Denver was much more than an entertainer. He believed that everyone can make a difference, so he put his feelings into action. Although he continued to sing until his death in 1997, in his later career John mostly campaigned for social and environmental causes, including Feed the Children, The Hunger Project, and Friends of the Earth.

Janeen Mason loves color, light, music, laughter, children, babies, animals, books, friends, diving, painting, cooking, travel, Scrabble, family, the oceans, and science—and it's all apparent in her bright, lively art. Mason's original paintings hang in the private collections of movie stars and her children's book illustrations are featured in a one-woman show exhibited in museums. She was appointed a Member on the Florida Arts Council where she advocates for arts and culture for everyone in Florida, from nursery schools to nursing homes. Her irresistible enthusiasm makes her a popular speaker at schools, libraries, and conferences. She says, "Adapting and illustrating this song by John Denver is a dream come true!"

ALSO IN THE JOHN DENVER & KIDS SERIES

Sunshine On My Shoulders

Ancient Rhymes: A Dolphin Lullaby

Take Me Home, Country Roads

Grandma's Feather Bed

Dawn Publications is dedicated to inspiring in children a deeper understanding and appreciation for all life on Earth. To review our titles or to order, please visit us a www.dawnpub.com, or call 800-545-7475.